W9-BBU-815

One Little Chicken

A COUNTING BOOK

by DAVID ELLIOTT

illustrated by ETHAN LONG

Holiday House / New York

To the flock on School Street: the Hanwells—Wendy, Scott, Allison, and Finn

D. E.

For Heather, Katherine, Cooper, and Carson. I love you with all my heart.
Now throw on the Dance Mix!

E. L.

Text copyright © 2007 by David Elliott
Illustrations copyright © 2007 by Ethan Long
All Rights Reserved
Printed and Bound in Malaysia
The art was created with the help of Mac and a little mouse.
The text typeface is Aunt Mildred.
www.holidayhouse.com
First Edition
1 3 5 7 9 10 8 6 4 2
Library of Congress Cataloging-in-Publication Data
Elliott, David (David A.), 1947–
One little chicken : a counting book / by David Elliott ; illustrated by Ethan Long. — 1st ed.
p. cm.
Summary: Watch the little chickens dance, while counting to ten by chance.
ISBN-13: 978-0-8234-1983-8 (hardcover)
[1. Chickens—Fiction. 2. Dance—Fiction. 3. Counting.
4. Stories in rhyme.] I. Long, Ethan, ill. II. Title.
PZ8.3.E4920n 2007
[E]—dc22
2006037046

1

One chicken
twirls like a top.

Two chickens do the bunny hop.

2

Three chickens
practice their ballet.

3

Four chickens
swing the night away.

4

Five chickens put on five grass skirts.

5

Then they hula
and they hula
and they hula
till it hurts.

Six chickens try something more refined.

6

But seven chickens
get up and bump and grind.

Eight chickens swirl
and sway in satin.

8

Nine chickens cha-cha
to a beat that's hot and Latin.

And ten chickens
shimmy shimmy
shimmy shimmy
shimmy shimmy
SHAKE!

10

But one little chicken
will not bugaloo.
Who is that little chicken?

So get up and shake a leg.
Strut your stuff and cut a rug.

Count to ten and back
as you jive and jitterbug.

Make your own music with wax paper and a comb

and dance! dance! dance!
till the cows come home.